Stories From Scotland

Edited By Vicki Skelton

First published in Great Britain in 2020 by:

 Young**Writers**® Est. 1991 —

Young Writers
Remus House
Coltsfoot Drive
Peterborough
PE2 9BF
Telephone: 01733 890066
Website: www.youngwriters.co.uk

Printed and bound in the UK by BookPrintingUK
Website: www.bookprintinguk.com
YB0450A

FOREWORD

Ladies and gentlemen, boys and girls, roll up roll up to see the weirdest and wackiest creations the world of fiction has ever seen!

Young Writers presents to you the wonderful results of *Ridiculous Writers*, our latest competition for primary school pupils. We gave them the task of creating a crazy combo to give them a character or an object around which they could base their story. They picked an adjective or verb and a noun at random and the result is some super creations, along with the added bonus of reinforcing their grammar skills in a fun and engaging way.

But the fun didn't end there, oh no! Once they had their subject they had to write a story, with the added challenge of doing it in just **100 words!** I think you'll agree they've achieved that brilliantly – this book is jam-packed with wacky and wonderful tales.

Here at Young Writers we want to pass our love of the written word onto the next generation and what better way to do that than to celebrate their writing by publishing it in a book! We believe their confidence and love of creative writing will grow, and hopefully these young writers will one day be the authors of the future. An absorbing insight into the imagination of the young, we hope you will agree that this amazing anthology is one to delight the whole family again and again.

CONTENTS

Loreburn School, Dumfries

Lilia McCallay (10)	52
Jessica Brown (10)	53
Siobhan Murray (8)	54
Heather Hornby (10)	55
Katie Brown (10)	56
Lilli Laurie (9)	57
Diana White (9)	58
Blythe Andie Wilson Murray (10)	59
Mckenzie Mcgarrie (10)	60
Marley Lord (9)	61
Millie Lawson (10)	62
Declan Jardine (9)	63
Beatrice Uzezi Okposio (9)	64
Lierra Kerr (9)	65
Logan McCluskey (9)	66

Onthank Primary School, Kilmarnock

Bradley Black (7)	67
Lola James (7)	68
Megan Wilson (7)	69
Sarah Gibson (7)	70
Lucy Hunter (7)	71
Lucas McAvoy (7)	72
Jay McFadzean (7)	73
Rachel McTaggart (7)	74
Blaine Prentice (7)	75
Sadie Farmer (7)	76
Ollie Toner (8)	77
Hannah Johnson (7)	78
Ruari Boyd (7)	79

Pentland Primary School, Edinburgh

Kory Palomino (8)	80
Sophie Ormiston (8)	81
Ellie Moss (8)	82
Ellie Banyard (8)	83
Aila Budu-Forson (8)	84
Flinn Handley (8)	85

Sophia Clutterbuck (8)	86
Alexander Rolland (8)	87
Robert Hagarty (8)	88
Reese Robertson (8)	89
Cara Bisset (8)	90
Ellie Lendrum (8)	91
Autumn Edgar (8)	92
Jayden Millar (8)	93
Eve McKenna (8)	94
Mohammad Ghanbari (8)	95
Otis Henderson (8)	96
Felicity Noble (8)	97
Conor Sheridan (8)	98

Preston Tower Primary School, Prestonpans

Olivia Fraser	99
Calvin McBrierty	100
Jay Brechin	101
Niamh Aldis (10)	102
Abby McKenzie (10)	103
Abigail Shearer	104
Daniel Cormack	105
Lucy Thomson (10)	106
Cody Murphy (10)	107
Cayden Lawson (10)	108
Fabiana Ferreira	109

St Mungo's RC Primary School, Alloa

Ala Mazurek (10)	110
Martin de Vries (10)	111
Eve Louise Blyth (10)	112
Jamie MacAskill (10)	113
Isla Mullan (10)	114
Matthew Little (10)	115
Samavia Javeed (9)	116
Lucy Barr (10)	117
Aidan Lambert (10)	118
Dima Clark (11)	119
Hannah McMillan (9)	120
Macy Ireland (10)	121

Thornwood Primary School, Glasgow

Hanin Alqarni (8)	122
Freya Stewart (9)	123
Cal Hanlon (9)	124
Iona Sherrington (8)	125
Robbie Sawatzky (8)	126
Aqsa Ahmad (8)	127
Stefanie Kokkinaki (9)	128
Logan Gow (8)	129
Ibrahim Nazir (8)	130
Kieran Alcorn (8)	131
Anna Marie McShane (9)	132
Nampreet Kaur Brar (8)	133
Mabel Elizabeth Gurney (8)	134
Harsimran Kaur Sohal (8)	135
Navneet Brar (9)	136
Matthew Fletcher (8)	137

Winton Primary School, Ardrossan

Teagan Jagger (12)	138

THE
STORIES

Me And Jonathan Got Sucked Into The Game

Jonathon and I were playing FIFA 20. Jonathon said, "I'm having fun." But then Jonathon said, "I need to do something."

"Okay." Suddenly I got sucked inside the game. I got scared a bit.

Jonathon came back and looked for me. Suddenly he got sucked into the game.

Then I saw something. I said, "I am going to get you."

Jonathon said, "You're going down."

So we were playing and Jonathon was passing everyone the ball but I got the ball and scored and we got transported and I said, "I am not doing that ever again."

Saied Kidamait (10)

All Saints Primary School, Airdrie

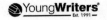

Mixable Earth

In the new new world, lived daft characters. They included Superman, Daft Banana and the clumsy chickens. They all were dumb in their own way. Superman kept removing the earth and his own body without knowing what he was doing! Chaos! Well, yes! Daft Banana had hundreds of children and ate all of them! He loves juicy... uh, juicy bananas. The clumsy chickens sat all day on top of each other, watching chicken shows... smelling their feet. All of them were good friends and they had one thing in common. They wore socks on their heads and were dumb.

Joshua Higgins (9)
All Saints Primary School, Airdrie

The Adventures Of Squid And Mr Popping Bottoms

Mr Popping Bottoms was alone so he went to El Capo restaurant. Mr Popping Bottoms ordered squid. He was about to eat it and then the squid was alive. It went, "La la la la!" And Mr Popping Bottoms began to be best friends with the squid. They went on adventures and they went swimming. Mr Popping Bottoms nearly drowned. Years passed by, Squid died and his gravestone said 'RIP. Loved by Mr Popping Bottoms forever and always'. Soon after, Mr Popping Bottoms saw Squid in Heaven. There, they continued all of their adventures.

Mia McDermid (10)
All Saints Primary School, Airdrie

3

Gracie's First Day At School

Summer had just ended and Gracie was getting nervous because it was time to start school. That morning, Gracie said to her mum, "Do I have to go to school?"

Her mum said, "No need to feel nervous. You are a smart, young, beautiful girl."

Gracie felt a bit better. She went to pack her bag and then ran to catch the bus.

When she got to school she went to meet her teacher. Her teacher was very nice. Her name was Miss Rose. Gracie then enjoyed school much more. She made two best friends, Katie and Emily.

Emily Grace Freel (9)

All Saints Primary School, Airdrie

Mr Freeze

One day in Scotland, Dr Gloom set Scotland on fire. No one noticed until in the freeze cave an emergency alert was signalled to Mr Freeze.
"Time to do my thing."
He went to Scotland as fast as he could. As he was putting out the fire he saw Dr Gloom. As he flew over to Dr Gloom, Dr Gloom whistled. It was very strange.
Zoom! A flying board flew over to him and then Dr Gloom flew away. Mr Freeze shot him with freeze guns and Dr Gloom froze.
Mr Freeze carried him away to jail and saved Scotland.

Nathan Mitchell Smith (9)
All Saints Primary School, Airdrie

5

The Monster That Cares

There was a monster called Theo. Theo was a lonely monster. That afternoon he fell in a puddle and got soaking wet.

Out of the blue, came a red and pink monster with beautiful love hearts spotted all over her. The pretty monster was called Rosy. She ran over to poor Theo lying in the puddle. Theo was relieved he could get a friend.

After a long time of thinking, Theo had the confidence to ask her what her name was. Rosy and Theo walked along happily. They smiled at each other. He wasn't lonely anymore. He was happy.

Mya McGhee (9)
All Saints Primary School, Airdrie

Nightmare

Today Mum showed me a website that said 'An asteroid is going to hit the Earth'. She said it was going to happen tomorrow. About a million thoughts went through my head. My best thought was a new species would be born.

It was almost night now and I was worried sick. It would happen in an hour. I could actually see it. It was enormous. Maybe I'd get moved to a different time zone but it was unlikely.

I'm as happy as can be. It was all a dream but then again, maybe it's time for a new species.

Jonathan McInnes (9)
All Saints Primary School, Airdrie

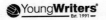

The World Of Cake

I was born on Venus. I went on my mum's spaceship to explore and I found a sponge consistency and a thick substance. It was an enormous ball. I landed and all of a sudden the ship started to sink. The door was covered so I smashed a window and jumped out. I landed in goop.
Luckily, I found a friend. He was red and circular. He had over 2,000 friends. I told them about my ship so they made me a ship out of them and put candles on their feet. I got home safely. Yay! Everyone missed me!

Anna Armitage (9)
All Saints Primary School, Airdrie

My 10th Birthday Party

It was a summer's day and it was my tenth birthday party. It was Hollywood ball themed and the dress code was fancy. I had a red carpet outside my door, all-you-can-eat sweets and a chocolate fountain. All my friends were invited. We danced all night, made a fort, ate lots of food and laughed at Rachel's jokes.

Then I woke up and checked the time. It was 3am on the 5th of March 2020. It actually wasn't my birthday. It was all a dream.

Jessica Pryce (9)
All Saints Primary School, Airdrie

Cucumber Castle

One day I was in a castle, a cucumber castle. I love cucumber so much. Everything was made out of cucumber.
I went on a walk for a long time. I came home and a little man was standing in front of my castle. He said, "We need to knock your castle down."
I was in shock, but they had to do what they had to do so I let him and we all ate the cucumber. It was all gone.

Abbie Wyllie (9)
All Saints Primary School, Airdrie

Ruby The Clumsy Robot

1900.

"It's alive!" shouted the scientist mischievously because right in front of him was a weird, friendly robot that he named Ruby. Now Ruby wasn't a normal robot because when she was made there was a system under load so she was clumsy. She was dangerous...

2020.

It's 15:34 and Ruby was in the lab by herself because the scientists were having lunch.

"It's party time..." Ruby whispered. Then suddenly an extraordinary bang formed into an eruption of flames in the lab all because Ruby knocked over a few chemicals. Luckily, nobody was injured but Ruby disappeared to clumsy camp.

Emily Barnes

Bushes Primary School, Glenburn

The Snotty Fairy

Fiona the fairy strolled upside down to the nauseating pub. Just outside, there was a sign reading: *Do not sniff for tarantulas* above some yellow blueberries. However, Fiona did just that. Then deep in her nostrils, something started pouring out. The stickiest, gooiest, grossest snot ever. Fiona bashed against the door and covered the dainty blossoming flower with snot. The bunny bartender tried to get Fiona out but didn't succeed until an avalanche enveloped everything, from a graffitied Mona Lisa to a misplaced grumbling toilet. Unfortunately nothing was salvageable from the pub of snot, not even the Mona Lisa.

Rachel Simpson (11)
Bushes Primary School, Glenburn

Disgusting Doctor Grizzo

One cold day in a hospital there was a doctor; his name was Doctor Grizzo. He was so evil that his co-workers were scared of him. He would bite bananas sideways. *Gasp!* He would bite into bubble tape. *Gasp!* He would scratch the chalkboard with his long nails. *Oh!*

But one day, a girl called Miss Manky came to prove that she was more evil than him. She came in and rubbed out everything on the whiteboard but left one small bit. *Ah!* She took out an ice cream and bit it!

"Aargh!" He jumped out the window.

Owen Waddell (11)
Bushes Primary School, Glenburn

The Lazy Ghost

It all started in 2016 when Suzy awoke from her coffin. However, unlike the other afterlife creatures, Suzy would just lie in her coffin, snoring away. As she was in a deep sleep Suzy was blissfully unaware that everyone else in the graveyard was out chasing anyone that dared to go in at night. Slowly, as she woke up she could see her daughter through the black coffin and wet earth. She was crying. Suzy tried to shout to her but she didn't hear. Soon after, she fell asleep. From then on Suzy was only awake three hours a day.

Aeryn Morris Devlin (11)
Bushes Primary School, Glenburn

The Evil Foot

One day, an evil foot was in the bathroom and got floated down the toilet by accident. When he was down in the sewer he was getting really excited about... biting his toenails. Also, he was excited to eat the fluff in between their toes which I say is very... just, eww. He spent about an hour or two down there.

He eventually came back up the drain from the bath with all the hair that felt like a spider's web. At least that's what he told me last month in Julember.

Leah Patterson (11)

Bushes Primary School, Glenburn

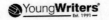

So Near But Yet So Far

It was a sunny day in Barcelona, it was very hot outside. It was meant to be ice cream day and Raspberry was waiting to be selected. A customer came and asked for the flavour vanilla. Vanilla was selling fast, Raspberry was feeling sad as he never got picked. They just kept coming and coming and he never got picked. Suddenly, a little boy wanted raspberry ice cream. He was finally picked, he had never been so excited! He waited and finally he got picked. He was just about to be eaten when... *plop!* He was dropped on the floor!

Tabitha Ward (10)
Denholm Primary School, Denholm

The Hairy Toilet

Once, there was a hairy toilet. Nobody wanted to sit on him. His beard was so scratchy that everyone got a rash on their bum! He became lonely because no one visited him. He began to cry. There was a barbershop next door. The barber heard crying. He searched high and low until he found out who was crying. "What's the matter?" "No one comes here anymore. I am too scratchy." The barber said, "I can shave your hair off!" "Yes please," said the toilet. Everyone used his toilet again. He was not lonely. "Yippee!"

Robbie Maitland (9)
Dunbog Primary School, Cupar

The Powerful Pizza

One day, there was a powerful pizza called Pepperoni. His mission was to destroy an important city - not just any city, but the city of London. He asked his friends to help destroy the city. Every powerful pepperoni pizza immediately agreed! They turned on their racing rims and whizzed through Westminster and the Tower of London. They went crazy and went super-duper fast!

Suddenly, Brave Broccoli arrived just before they reached Buckingham Palace. He detected them and destroyed them. He was the hero of the day. The Queen came out of the palace and knighted him, Sir Broccoli!

Isla Moss (9)
Dunbog Primary School, Cupar

Gullible Gangster

There was a gullible gangster. He lived on a scary street. He had a nosy neighbour. Fudge the gangster bought CCTV. He saw a scary man. He knocked on the door. "Hello, my name is Fudge."
"Got that! Why are you so nosy?"
"I am very lonely."
Snigger!
"Can you give me a lift to the shop?" Gullible Fudge believed him and drove to the shop.
They arrived home with a trolley full of fudge. They emptied them on the floor.
"Ha ha! I am not lonely! I just like eating fudge... yum!"

Levi Johnstone (10)
Dunbog Primary School, Cupar

Terrible Toilet

Once, there was a hungry toilet who ate people!
One day, a ghost arrived. The ghost was as light as
a feather so the toilet did not notice him and did
not eat him. The ghost brought all of his ghost
friends to the cubicle. No one came to the toilet
because it was haunted.
The toilet got hungrier and hungrier. He was so
weak that with his final effort he squirted some of
the disgusting toilet water onto the ghosts. They
promised never to haunt the toilet again if he
didn't eat people. They 'lived' happily ever after.

Lucas Smith (8)
Dunbog Primary School, Cupar

The Wicked Teacher

The wicked teacher called Miss Evil was in the classroom holding a whip, telling the children they would be whipped if they didn't do all their maths. She was so mad she left the class and the kids plotted to find her whip. They found a locked metal box under her desk with the key still in the padlock. Eventually, they got into the box and found the whip.

The teacher came into the class ten minutes later and all the kids were shocked as she had changed into a kind, helpful teacher. They were all happy and cheered loudly.

Jakob McSorley (10)
Dunbog Primary School, Cupar

The Predator

A low growl could be heard. The rumble came from deep within, like a storm approaching. With milky grey eyes like miniature moons, the cat began to prowl steadily out the tall grass, examining Alex from head to toe. He was terrified. He didn't know what to do. He tried to run but his body froze. No matter how hard he tried he couldn't move! Then before Alex even had time to process what was happening, it pounced! All that could be heard was a deep squelch of the leopard's teeth finding a home in Alex's torso.

Oscar Edward Rawlings (12)
Dunbog Primary School, Cupar

Spooky Scientist

There was a spooky scientist. He had no friends. He was so lonely; he only spoke to his pet hamster. Suddenly, there was an explosion and the scientist appeared clutching the hamster. The scientist had no clothes on! He made a spell to make new clothes but when he wore them his face, arms and legs were all mixed up.

The hamster ran off and brought back some neighbours. They all felt sorry for the scientist. He was never lonely again. He had learned a valuable lesson - never try to make friends, let them come to you!

Charlotte Ferguson (9)
Dunbog Primary School, Cupar

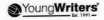
Hairy Pizza

Once, there was a silly scientist who lived in a luxury lab! He liked eating pepperoni pizza. He spilled a hair-growing potion on his pizza. He picked the pizza up, rushed into his lab and tried to fix it! He knocked a 'come alive' potion on to it. The pizza grew a beard and legs and arms appeared. Suddenly it ran out of the building and down the street! The pizza took the 'come alive' potion to the pizza shop. He poured the potion on his pizza friends. They all grew arms and legs. They had a pizza party!

Ellis Stuart (9)
Dunbog Primary School, Cupar

The Hairy Pizza

Bob was making a pizza when suddenly his beard started to fall out all over the pizza. He chucked the pizza in the bin.

In the middle of the night, the bin started rattling and out stepped a very hairy, yucky pizza. It found Bob in his bedroom fast asleep. The pizza wanted revenge so it picked up Bob, took him downstairs and flung Bob in the bin.

The next day, Bob heard a loud crashing noise as the bin was tipped upside down. He smelt the foulest smell ever and realised he was being tipped into the bin lorry!

Katie Wilson (11)
Dunbog Primary School, Cupar

The Hungry Doctor

Doctor Locuse was always focused. One day, he forgot breakfast so when a patient came Doctor Locuse ate the infection on her ear and she left without an itch! The next patient had a tummy rash but with a quick gasp, the patient found there was no more rash. Locuse had eaten it. Locuse was still hungry. The next patient had man flu. Locuse took a blood sample but there was nothing wrong with him! But Locuse already ate it. Then he had an ear infection and a rash on his tummy, but nobody could see what was wrong.

Louise Janet Brooks (11)
Dunbog Primary School, Cupar

The Mean Plant

There was a mean plant called Mr Farty. No one went close to him because he smelt disgusting, just like a skunk. It did not rain and the plant got drier and drier. He almost shrivelled away to nothing! He could not even cry!

A lady saw him. She had green fingers! She put a clothes peg on her nose. She filled a watering can and edged closer to him. The water saved the plant and not only that, it turned him into the sweetest smelling flower around. Soon, he had lots of friends and was called Mr Scent!

Lexie Smith (9)
Dunbog Primary School, Cupar

The Hairy Pizza

Once upon a time, there was a bald man that went to the hairdressers to make his hair grow back. He brought a pizza with him and sat down on the chair and the hairdresser started to pour some hair growing potion on the man's head. But he spilt a bit and it fell on the pizza and the pizza began to grow hair. Not before long, it became very hairy. It became known as the hairy pizza and everyone wanted a hairy pizza. Soon, pizza all over the world became sold out and the hairdresser became very rich.

Hannah Gourley (10)
Dunbog Primary School, Cupar

The Fierce Football

The fierce football was on the pitch. The goalkeeper kicked the ball so hard it went flying into the crowd! The fierce football was now ferocious and came flying back. Everyone ducked and ran for cover! The goalie phoned the police and they sent a detective! He could not see anything wrong until the ball smacked him right on the nose! It was like the ball had come alive. It had a mouth, arms and legs. Luckily, the detective played rugby. He tackled the ball to the ground and managed to deflate him.

Jake Pickard
Dunbog Primary School, Cupar

The Nervous Ninja

There was a nervous ninja. Every time he trained he was clumsy. His master made him a series of tasks. First, he had to knock down a wall. He was so clumsy he collided with it. Next, he was sent on a spy mission. He burned his hand and let out a loud "Ouch!" which alerted the guy!

The final task was to go to the dangerous dungeon and set all the ninjas free. He crept towards the keys but tripped and landed on the guard who arrested him and locked him up with all the other ninjas.

Philip Matusiewicz (9)
Dunbog Primary School, Cupar

Gangsta Ghost

Hi, I am a ghost. I do gangsta stuff. I once stole the Crown Jewels. We never got caught as we were invisible!

One day, I stole a car from a bloke. He thought he could smell something but too late! I was so successful I decided to steal a jumbo jet. However, just as I was creeping inside the cockpit I made a terrible smell. It was disgusting. This time everyone smelled me! The smell was so strong it knocked me out. In fact, I was turned into vapour! Oh well - it was fun while it lasted!

Madison Woods (9)

Dunbog Primary School, Cupar

Heads

There was once a teacher who wanted an eye on the back of her head so she could keep an eye on her students. She went to the deep dark city where the great wizard lived. She went to his house. The old man let her in. The nervous teacher walked in and told him what she wanted to happen. He mumbled a little and waved his hands about. Then suddenly she had two heads instead of an eye on the back of her head. The great wizard did not know what to do, so she left with two heads.

Anna Mountain (11)
Dunbog Primary School, Cupar

Kev And The Dolls

Hi, I'm Kev. My story is a bit strange! I was playing Roblox in my bedroom at 12pm when there was a bang on my door. I slowly opened it to see a weird woman with warts all over her face! She was holding six dolls. Then immediately she disappeared. The dolls lay on the ground in a heap. I picked them up.

The next day, wedding bells were ringing and I was meant to be getting married. Instead, the dolls and I were playing Roblox. Even worse, the dolls were winning.

Grace Millar (8)
Dunbog Primary School, Cupar

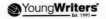
Lego Island

It was a normal day on Lego Island but I stepped out of line and wanted to be free. So I ran for the nearest plane and I was about to get on when the security caught me.

The next day, I was heading for the toilet when I saw a helicopter land so I took my chance again and this time I actually got in the helicopter. Then I had to find the right switches. Once that was done, all I had to do was take off and that's exactly what I did. Up and away, into the sky.

Archie Pickard (10)
Dunbog Primary School, Cupar

The Circus In Need

Once, a man called Tim Morris had a circus that was shutting down in two days. The day before shutting down a man went to his house and said, "I have got a surprise for you." He led him to his van and gave him centaurs, flying elephants, acrobatic sausages and a shape-shifting baby. Two years later, he was earning £2,000,000 a month. Then he made an announcement that they were going on tour and then he became the richest man in the world.

Zak Healy (11)
Fintry Primary School, Dundee

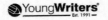

The Intimidated Curry Stain

So it all began in a small Indian restaurant when a little boy spilt his curry and it wouldn't come out. So they had to find the magical anti-curry stain remover! Quickly, the family started to panic. They didn't want to climb the massive chappati mountain but they realised they couldn't let the curry stain eat the little boy's shirt. So they set off up the mountain.

It was a lonely and stressful two days before they finally reached the high peak but when they got there the curry stain punched the stain remover but eventually was killed.

Thomas Hair (11)
Inverkip Primary School, Inverkip

The Murderous Pencil

The murderous pencil was a pencil that was always destroying all the paper with its sharp and clever tactics to cover it up. But the rubbers didn't like this pencil and thought that he should be stopped. But they could never catch him.

One day, the rubbers fought back against the pencil and prepared all of their best rubbers. The rubbers and the pencil fought hard. The rubbers found the pencil and charged at it but the pencil moved like someone from the Matrix and stabbed all of the rubbers. The rubbers retreated. The pencil won.

John-Nicolai Hunt (11)
Inverkip Primary School, Inverkip

Gangster Toilet

Never to be caught. Robbing banks and stealing jars. Comes from some land and flushes away. Never to be sat on or stay down. A grey flush and a dazzling gutter. The wealthiest toilet on Earth. Today's mission was to break into an ice cream parlour then the public toilet, looking for scraps. Up and away he flew. As everyone needed the loo. As soon as he got there he felt not a worry as he shouted, "Stay back everyone." With a flash of lightning and a magic star, he robbed the parlour and still has never been caught.

Ava Miller (11)
Inverkip Primary School, Inverkip

The Farting Water

Somewhere near an empty lake, a man with farting water in a jar in a tub in a basket in a car was driving along to dispose of the water when it started to rain. The rain got heavier and heavier and heavier until thunder appeared. Driving up the hill (to the lake) into the clouds, the water farted so much that the lids on the jar, tub, basket and door flew open and the man jumped out. The car kept going into the thunder and lightning. Then rolling down the hill, went a tyre.

Lewis McDonald (11)

Inverkip Primary School, Inverkip

The Twisted Cinderella Story

Oh no! Cinderella is ugly but her stepsisters have taken her beauty. Drama is building up. The ugly stepmother is still ugly. She wants to be like her daughters but she can't. She snatches the fairy godmother's wand right out her hand to make herself beautiful.

They all arrive at the palace, waiting for the prince. Cinderella is stuck at home cleaning. The stepsisters and stepmother are battling over the prince. Weirdly enough, the stepmother gets to be with him and marries him, despite the forty-year age gap. He is twenty and she is sixty. This story is crazy!

Nicole Wood (11)

Kennoway Primary School, Kennoway

Food People

One morning, Anna was reading the newspaper and found a man had turned into a doughnut! There were other crazy cases - some turned into pizza, macaroni and sandwiches. Anna went to a scientist and asked how people were turning into food. He said it was because people were eating too much of the same food! Anna really liked cheese and her mum really liked crackers, but they thought nothing of it.

Suddenly her dad turned into a glass of beer! Then straight after that, Anna turned into cheese and her mum turned into crackers. Then they got eaten by giants!

Iqra A Asif (11)
Kennoway Primary School, Kennoway

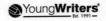
Father And Son's Crazy Adventures

There once lived a boy called Julian October and he sadly had no siblings or a mother but he had a dad called Max. They lived in a small house and Max didn't have a job and he was very very silly! When Julian was three he wanted a Happy Meal from McDonald's but Max went to the chippy and got him a doner kebab that was bigger than him! Max said, "Son, I have something to tell you."

"Dad, what is it?"

"I got you from the adoption centre."

"So I'm adopted?!"

Max went to jail.

Max Buist (12)
Kennoway Primary School, Kennoway

Time Travelling

Three young teenagers were in the Sahara Desert. They had been walking for some time now. They finally decided to have a break but someone noticed something in the distance... It looked like a tall square box which had dark colours! They decided to check it out. On the outside, it spelt 'telephone box'. They agreed that two people should go into the box because three would be too many. The two people went in... After a few minutes, the last person went to check the other people but they were gone! They looked everywhere but they were not seen!

Hope Goodlad (11)
Kennoway Primary School, Kennoway

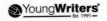
The Day Raheem's Life Changed Forever...

On a very strange Saturday, City were playing Wycombe Wanderers in the FA Cup. The ball was played to Sterling and, as usual, he ran in his unique running style. But then... a meteor hit him! He now looked like Akinfenwa - he was now using the earthquake style. *Boom! Boom! Boom!* And Akinfenwa was like a stickman and running like he just came out of Asda with his shopping bags! It was on this bizarre day these men's lives changed forever - the end is yet to be known... But there might be another day in the future, who knows? Nobody!

Cameron Murray (11)
Kennoway Primary School, Kennoway

The Great Escape

There was once an animal jail where all the naughty animals went. There was often a guard but not a normal guard... he was different! He always went "Woof!"

Then one day at lunchtime, the guard took one of the dogs and told him he was there to get them free. The next day there was a big explosion! Alarms were ringing and the animals were running for the exits! Outside the jail there were mountains all around them. The dog guard was waiting with three helicopters... And that's how it happened... The great animal escape!

Ethan Page (11)

Kennoway Primary School, Kennoway

The Bakery Disaster!

There once was a bakery that enticed the customers as soon as they walked in. One day, a man walked in with the most disgusted look on his face and shouted, "Eww!" then left! Well, the bakery owner was appalled by this so he shouted at his pastries and asked them to smell better! The pastries listened and the next day everyone was walking in and wafting the smell to their noses, but then they would pass out on the floor! The bakery owner was so confused by this but then he realised it was because of the disgusting stench.

Eilidh Simpson (12)
Kennoway Primary School, Kennoway

The Private Island

Jeff, Jimmy and Karen went on holiday to their private holiday house. Once they got there an earthquake hit the water. It was said that there would be a tsunami. Its might would hit their island and if it did the volcano would erupt.

Two hours later, the tsunami hit... They went to a bunker.

When they came out the whole island was covered in ice cream. The volcano was going to erupt again so Jeff, Jimmy and Karen called the coast guard to save them! He didn't come because it was a private island so they had to stay.

Mikey Bell (11)

Kennoway Primary School, Kennoway

The Egg Called Eck!

Once on a very very hot summer's day in Edinburgh, Eck was happily skipping down the street listening to music on his headphones. He came to a road. Eck didn't see the cars coming and how fast they were going so he crossed. Soon he was lying on the floor. He was split in half, yolking all of his yolk out of him. He had split in half!
A couple of weeks later, Eck's friends planned a funeral with Alex Little's Funerals. The funeral was two weeks after the scene. It was devastating.

Abi-Lee Lindsay (11)
Kennoway Primary School, Kennoway

Banana Busters

Once upon a time, there was a regular man going to a top-notch security prison. The man had a dog, Sir Barkenton. They were on their way when *crash!* Thunder came flying down! Ethan, the man, was merged with a banana so he became Peely! Sir Barkenton was merged with a bomb so he became Nuke Dog!

Our heroes were put in jail but... Peely had a plan! They put it into action and busted out. They went on to go on more adventures but went on to also make friends like Dog Guard.

Rocco Milne (11)

Kennoway Primary School, Kennoway

The Monsters' Disco

This story starts in 2014, based in LA. Mike Wisowski and his friends were watching TV and they saw an advert about a disco night and one of Mike's friends wanted them to go. But they didn't know what age you had to be. Mike and his friends went on an adventure to the disco to see if there was a poster that said what age you had to be to be able to go in. They trotted down the road to then find out that they were old enough to go to it. They were monsters.

Liam Bruce (12)
Kennoway Primary School, Kennoway

The Wolf Who Cried Boy

Once upon a time, there was a house with a grassy field in a town called Kennoway. There was a wolf that lied all the time.

It was a sunny day and there was a wolf who lived in the house with his family. When the wolf looked out of the window he found something strange... There was a person who was trying to kill the sheep! The person killed all the sheep and the wolf was scared. The wolf promised his mum and dad that he would never lie again.

Michael Van Rooyen (11)
Kennoway Primary School, Kennoway

The Hairy Pizza

"Mum, I want a pizza from that weird new shop!" I cried.
"Well order it then!" Mum replied.
So I ordered my pizza. It came a few minutes later. I opened the box, horrified. "That pizza's hairy!" I screamed.
"Are you sure? I think it might just be spinach," said Mum.
"Well I didn't ask for spinach, did I!"
"Well, are you hungry or not?" asked Mum.
I picked up the pizza. The pizza screamed, "I don't want to be eaten! I only went to that shop because I thought I was going to Madrid! Goodbye! And I am hairy."

Lilia McCallay (10)
Loreburn School, Dumfries

The Evil Pirate Bunny

"Yo ho yo ho, a sailor's life for me..."
On a ship on the coast of Spain, there are sailors celebrating. They are singing, dancing, even farting to the songs. They are singing but suddenly they see a shadow. They all freeze. Everyone is silent, although you can hear a mouse squeak. So not everyone.
Then a pirate bunny comes in. Suddenly he farts. Everyone passes out. The bunny laughs, "Wah ha ha!" He runs out into the dead of night, planning his next move - to take over the world. Everything is silent again. There's no sound. Nothing!
Then *fart!*

Jessica Brown (10)
Loreburn School, Dumfries

Cathie Cucumber's Highland Fling

An excited Cathie set out on her adventure from Dumfries in Andrew Murray's big, shiny fruit and vegetable lorry to meet her friends, Charlie and Chelsea, in Glasgow. They planned to go to the Nevis Highland Dance Festival in Fort William. From Glasgow they hiked up the famous West Highland Way, sleeping in a tent at night (creepy) and watching out for stags and the Hogwarts Express.

In Fort William, they met up with Tommy Tomato, Susan Strawberry, Grant Grape and Kree Kiwi. They had a great time at the festival and to everyone's surprise, won the cup! Yippee!

Siobhan Murray (8)
Loreburn School, Dumfries

The Bogeyman

One stormy night, I had a bad dream about me going on a trip with the bogeyman to Bogey Land. I had to wake up! My bedroom was filled with bogeys! Maybe they were all fake.

"I have to wake up," I said to myself. "Stop panicking, just stop panicking! Aargh! Get me out of here!"

A bogey person arrived. "Eww, you're disgusting. Bless you, oh sorry," the bogey man said. "I think you're turning green like me. You're so green! Let's call you Snotty Zoe. I have to go home. Bye."

I wonder where he went next?

Heather Hornby (10)
Loreburn School, Dumfries

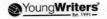

The Pretty Potato

I was walking through Tesco one day when I saw a potato. In fact, a very pretty potato indeed. I whipped out my camera and attempted to take a photo of this pretty potato but the potato just looked at me and said, "I'm tired of the paparazzi, darling!" then pirouetted out of the aisle into the make-up aisle. The potato tried out all the lipstick then dashed to the nail polish. Pretty Potato grabbed a trolley then smuggled all the nail polish out of the shop. "Ooh la la, darling!" screamed the potato. "I will be back."

Katie Brown (10)
Loreburn School, Dumfries

The Crazy Pizza

One day there was a pizza called Mr Crazy. The next day, Mr Crazy ran out of bed, forgetting to put his clothes on. So he put them on after his shower then he went to a park. It was super sunny. Mr Crazy saw a grey thing. It was his shadow but he never knew that. So he ran away from his shadow. Everyone was laughing at him.

"Stop!" said Mr Crazy. "What is this thing?" Mr Crazy shouted.

"It's your shadow," said a little girl.

"Oh," said Mr Crazy. "I am so crazy. Now I know that, bye."

Lilli Laurie (9)
Loreburn School, Dumfries

The Lazy Pizza!

One day in the pizza place it was a really busy day. It was shooting by, pizzas were getting made fast and soon Lazy Pizza was made. Soon after, the pizza was... alive! It was talking too. It said, "Hey! You are not going to take me anywhere, no, no, no."

Jeff was not happy to deliver this pizza! "Oh no!" On the way there, Jeff was on the highway and the pizza fell out of the box.

"Ummm..." Jeff said. Finally, Jeff arrived at Mrs Popple's house to deliver it.

"Sir, I don't like this."

Diana White (9)
Loreburn School, Dumfries

Gangsta Foot Sneaks Into Stomp Palace

Gangsta Foot gets out of prison with Naughty Stompy. They head off to Stomp Palace to steal the crown.

As they get in, Naughty Stompy trips up and guards come rushing after him. But Gangsta Foot hides and doesn't get found.

Gangsta Foot climbs up the stairs. Suddenly he farts and more of the same guards come up. Gangsta Foot hides behind a vase so the guards don't find him.

Gangsta Foot almost gets the crown but Queen Toes comes in and sees Gangsta Foot and says, "We will get you back in prison, Gangsta Foot!"

Blythe Andie Wilson Murray (10)

Loreburn School, Dumfries

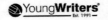
Hungry And Rude Toilet

When Josh wakes up he needs a dump so he goes to do his business. When he sits on the toilet it screams, "Oh, hairy and warm bum!" So Josh runs downstairs. Then the toilet says, "I'm hungry."
As it turns to night, the toilet goes into the kitchen and empties the fridge into its hole.
The next morning, Josh's mum needs a wee so she goes to sit on the toilet but it's not there! So she looks and finds it in the living room. She shakes it and the toilet says, "Rude, I'm trying to sleep."

Mckenzie Mcgarrie (10)
Loreburn School, Dumfries

The Smelly Teletubby

Stinky Winky Teletubby was minding his business walking to the Teletubby dump with his Teletubby friends. When they all got to the dump they went straight to the toilet ball pit. Once they got to the toilet ball pit there was a big scary spider playing in the ball pit. The Teletubbies were terrified so they asked the scary spider if they could play in the ball pit. The spider said, "Yes! Come on in." "Okay," said the Teletubbies. So the Teletubbies went into the ball pit. Yay!

Marley Lord (9)
Loreburn School, Dumfries

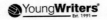

Piggly Jenner!

One day, Pig felt very bland so he went to find something to do. He went into the farmer's wife's room. He found something incredible! It was make-up! Pig tried it on. He was so excited he tried on a dress and high heels and... fake nails! Pig looked amazing so he went out to show the other animals. Pig somersaulted up to Goat. "What do you think?" Goat loved it! Pig asked all the other animals. They all loved it as well. From that day on, Pig was known as Piggly Jenner!

Millie Lawson (10)
Loreburn School, Dumfries

Paul Poo Saves The Day

Paul Poo woke up to save the day and he jumped in his fart mobile. Soon he fought Jeff Man. Next, he got Cow Freak. After that, he got caught up with *dun, dun, dun...* Bigfoot. He was not very strong so Paul Poo just farted on him. Later, he bumped into Farting Frizz blowing up Fart Land Bank. Oh no! He got right there. Suddenly, as quick as a blink of an eye he took the fart gun off her and ran away so fast across the whole world not even Flash could catch him and he was gone.

Declan Jardine (9)
Loreburn School, Dumfries

Evil Brother

There was an evil brother in the street and the evil brother gassed on his bed and he said that he would gas again. His mother said, "Do not destroy my picture." But he didn't listen. So then he decided to leave the house. He ran away and was making an evil plan to scare people and that was not good. His mother was worried about her son. One day his mother went out to the market and she saw him and she said, "Come, come, son. Come with me."

Beatrice Uzezi Okposio (9)
Loreburn School, Dumfries

The Terrible Trumping Teddy

One day I was in my room, minding my own business when I heard this terrible trumping noise coming from my closet. I went to go see what it was but nothing was in it but my brand-new teddy. I picked it up and gave it a hug but then my hand got hot. It was my teddy farting. But just then my feet lifted off the ground and then *whoosh!* I flew out the window into the sky with my teddy's fart. Then he took me to farting heaven to be the god that I am today.

Lierra Kerr (9)
Loreburn School, Dumfries

The Crazy Superhero

One day Adin was on the couch when the bank was getting robbed so he went in the bank but instead he robbed the bank too! Then he helped the other robber escape. The cop searched for weeks. Then they found them but they escaped from the cops.

Then they found them again and took them to prison. They regretted robbing the bank. They had to eat beans on toast for breakfast, lunch and dinner. Then they broke out of jail and never got found again.

Logan McCluskey (9)
Loreburn School, Dumfries

Forgetful Wizard

One day, four people walked down the road. They said, "Look! Let's go to that shop."
"Okay."
"Who is that? Let's say hi."
"What are you doing?"
"I will turn you into a Jaffa Cake."
"No!"
"Yes. In 3, 2, 1! Ha ha ha!"
"Help!"
"I will eat you!"
"No! Please!"
"Yes! 3, 2, 1... Yuck!" The four people were gone. "Wahaha!" the wizard said. "Yum! They were so good! Wahaha!"
It was on the TV. The police were looking for the wizard but he was nowhere to be seen.

Bradley Black (7)
Onthank Primary School, Kilmarnock

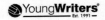
The Hairy Chef

I woke up and went downstairs for breakfast. I told my mum I was never going back to school ever again. She said, "Why?"
"Because of the chef. He has so much hair and it always goes in the food."
"It doesn't matter," said Mum. "Hurry up, the bus is here. I don't have time to make you a packed lunch, okay!"
"Okay, class, settle down. It's lunch!"
"Nooo!" I went and I got water and stew. It had lots of hairs.
I gave him a Christmas gift of a shaver and he shaved his beard. No hairs. Yippee!

Lola James (7)
Onthank Primary School, Kilmarnock

The Crazy Teacher And Her Crazy Kids

Once upon a time, there was a crazy teacher that taught children, crazy children. The kids threw paper kites at each other and sometimes at the teacher. It made her go crazy.

Then the next day it was the teacher's birthday. The teacher walked into a surprise. The kids jumped out from under their seats and shouted, "Surprise! Happy birthday!" They took all day giving her presents. She was so happy but there was something she wanted more than presents. She wanted the class to do work without throwing things and the kids were good in the end.

Megan Wilson (7)
Onthank Primary School, Kilmarnock

The Super Magical Dinosaur

Meet Max, an awesome boy that is a dinosaur who fights bad guys and girls.

One day, smoke unleashed. Evil was on the loose. Then he released that he was late for school! So he ran and ran then *bash!* He broke the school wall! He was in big trouble!

Oh no! Evil robots were here! It was time to fight. The robots were strong. "Uh oh!" Max got knocked out bad so he could not fight any longer. So could this be the end? Max said, "I need your help! Choose anything, just help me!" Then Max healed up.

Sarah Gibson (7)
Onthank Primary School, Kilmarnock

The Burping Rabbit

One day, two rabbits were out to play but one said, "I have a tummy ache." So they went back home. The rabbit was lying on his bed but then he burped and he kept burping till he couldn't stop. Then he went to the park and he burped in his friend's face. Yuck! So he ran away. The rabbit said, "I really want to get the burps away." So he tried and tried but they never went away. His brother said they would go away themselves. A few days later, they went away so the rabbit said, "Yes!"

Lucy Hunter (7)
Onthank Primary School, Kilmarnock

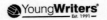

Clumsy Jeff Brother

There was a little boy called Jeff, he was walking in the city. His music turned off, his Wi-Fi turned off. He saw two big builders with lots of Wi-Fi. He climbed and climbed and fell again. He fell and fell and fell then he realised his shoelace was untied but he didn't know how to tie his shoelace! He fell again and Jeff said, "I don't know what I am doing." He got up and he could not get the Wi-Fi so he went to the top of the building and... fell! He went to the hospital then home.

Lucas McAvoy (7)
Onthank Primary School, Kilmarnock

The Grumbling Ninja

One scary night, a ninja got an alert on his super cool ninja watch. There was a robbery at the bank. Then he ran down the stairs and opened his door and hopped into his Porsche. He pressed the button to make the engine blast away and in one minute he was at the bank.

He rushed into the bank. The robber was a doll and he'd taken the most precious and rarest diamonds in the world. The ninja ran and did a front flip to get through the lasers, went to the next floor and got the robber.

Jay McFadzean (7)

Onthank Primary School, Kilmarnock

The Clumsy Fairy

There was a girl called Kate and she had a fairy called Lucy. She was clumsy and every night Kate and Lucy talked. But Kate had a nosy brother who spied on them. Then Kate's brother stayed in her bedroom for the night to see what she was up to. He found out she had a fairy and her brother told her mum because they would get into big trouble. The next night, he heard a noise so he looked out the window and he saw Lucy the fairy. She had a broken wing and then she disappeared.

Rachel McTaggart (7)
Onthank Primary School, Kilmarnock

Rude Superhero Jake

One morning, someone shouted his name and he said, "Shut up!" He was tired and grumpy. He was really rude and grumpy and was a really bad superhero but that's not all, he was a bad saver. He wanted to sit down and eat. He was lazy. He did not want to save people. He wanted to have his own way, but he never did. That is why he was so grumpy. He hated a lot of things, like cacti. But he loved dogs and cats. He was really lazy and he wanted to watch TV every day.

Blaine Prentice (7)
Onthank Primary School, Kilmarnock

The Messy Fairy

One day there was a little girl. She was called the messy fairy. She lived with her parents. She was messy because she messed up the house. She put make-up all over the furniture. She got into trouble. She had to go to detention. She got hurt by the boys when she was about to talk to the teacher. She brought her magic wand and she cast a spell and the boys got scared. They ran away to their houses and they got pillows and put it on their heads. The messy fairy went home.

Sadie Farmer (7)
Onthank Primary School, Kilmarnock

The Super Evil Robot

Once upon a time, there was a man. His name was Jack but then a man took him away and then the man turned Jack into Temhater. Now Temhater was evil. He had laser eyes, sharp teeth, sticky feet and claws. Temhater picked the man up and threw him to the ground and stepped on him. Then he laughed but the man had a ring which took him to Robot Land but they were good robots. So he destroyed them but then he found Temhater and they fought. But then Temhater was destroyed.

Ollie Toner (8)
Onthank Primary School, Kilmarnock

The Hungry Scientist

One day there was a scientist. It was a hungry scientist. All she did was eat. Then she discovered that candy had a lot of sugar so she went looking for candy. She found a lot of candy and she went to a lot of shops. Then she went back to where she was last time and she put it in a special machine. There was a lot of sugar. So she started a candy shop. She had a lot of customers. She had a lot of money and she spent the money on candy and it was so yummy.

Hannah Johnson (7)
Onthank Primary School, Kilmarnock

Evil Robot

The first morning I woke up and I heard a strange sound so I went down the stairs and I saw a robot. It was shooting lasers and one almost hit me but it went behind me and hit my mum. Then my dad came in the room and punched the robot in the arm. The arm came off and the robot's arm started to shoot lasers.

Ruari Boyd (7)
Onthank Primary School, Kilmarnock

The Farty Toilet

Once, a little child told his mum, "Mum! I have an emergency! I need to poo!"
"Go to the toilet in the bathroom."
"Where's the bathroom?"
"In India."
"Where's India?"
"You should know where India is." But she bought him his toilet.
The boy pooed. "Ah, I can finally poo. Wait, what's that smell? I think my toilet smells."
He found a letter that said 'this toilet farts really badly'. He sold the toilet but the person who bought it farted and the farts smelt like rotten flowers and it farted again!

Kory Palomino (8)
Pentland Primary School, Edinburgh

The Poorly Toilet!

One sunny day, there was a toilet. He was very poorly but he loved being flushed. Unfortunately, nobody flushed him. He was miserable. Suddenly the sink started to talk. He said, "Hey, toilet dude, how are you?"

The toilet said he was miserable because nobody would flush him. "Hey, can you flush me, Sink?" shouted the toilet.

The sink screamed and said, "No! I love seeing you miserable."

Day by day, the toilet grew sadder and sadder. Suddenly, the toilet's flush broke and then Toilet became moody. The sink had so much fun watching him.

Sophie Ormiston (8)
Pentland Primary School, Edinburgh

The Rotten Rabbit

Once upon a time, there were really nice rabbits and then they discovered a rotten rabbit. The rotten rabbit came out and fought the nice rabbits. The nice rabbits said, "Sorry for stalking you. We wanted to say hi to you to be polite and kind." Then the rotten rabbit said, "Oh, it's okay. I am a bit rotten and rude. I also like to fight. So sorry." "It's okay," said the nice rabbits. "You're nice. You're forgiven. You're not rotten anymore. You can stay in Nice Ville forever and ever and ever."

Ellie Moss (8)
Pentland Primary School, Edinburgh

The Silly Hairy Tooth

One day in a peaceful little house there was a big scream, "My tooth!" someone said. "It is ugly. I will not get any money for this thing! Put it in the bin."
"No, Amy, we will not. It is your tooth. It was in your mouth."
"Aargh! Give me a drink now!"
"No! We are not your slaves."
The tooth ran out of the bathroom, met another tooth and fell in love. They went to the tooth factory and got married and had kids. They were very rich and had great jobs. They lived a happy life.

Ellie Banyard (8)
Pentland Primary School, Edinburgh

The Hairy Hot Chocolate

One day, there was a bored little girl who asked her mum if they could go out and get a hot chocolate. But her mum said no because there was hot chocolate in the cupboard. So she went to the kitchen and got out the hot chocolate. It said 'Hairy Hot Chocolate. One scoop and hair will grow'. She didn't care so she put three scoops in. When it was done she popped it in and hair started to grow. She tried to make it stop but she couldn't. The hot chocolate said, "Can we be friends?" She said, "Yes."

Aila Budu-Forson (8)
Pentland Primary School, Edinburgh

Poop Invasion

One day, a guy called Fred went to the moon and then he got attacked by poops and turned into one. Then they knew there was life on Earth so they attacked Earth. One billion people turned into them and only a few people survived and destroyed one out of three fleets, so you can tell they were powerful. Then another fleet came. Then there were only three people who weren't poops. Although they were cute they were deadly. Just saying. Now they had a bat in one hand and a gun in the other. Then they got destroyed forever.

Flinn Handley (8)
Pentland Primary School, Edinburgh

The Poorly Toilet With An Unknown Skill

Once, there was an ordinary toilet. One day, someone came into the toilets with plastic. They couldn't be bothered to find a bin. They dumped it into the toilet.

The next day, the toilet was very ill. An hour later, a cookie came rolling into the bathroom. The cookie had a bite taken out of it. Then a chicken nugget came in but the weird thing was that it had legs. They both asked how he was but the toilet's pipes started to tingle. Then before they knew it, he was a foot. How silly can a toilet be?

Sophia Clutterbuck (8)
Pentland Primary School, Edinburgh

Toilet Adventure

One day a stupid toilet thought he was a cat. He went around saying, "I am a cat. I am a cat."
A boy saw him and he said, "Is that a talking toilet with arms?"
The toilet went home. He had been burgled. The burglar stole an important thing to him.
The next day, the toilet set off to search. He searched around the whole Earth. He was so annoyed.
The next morning, he set off again. He searched the whole Earth again and again and again and again and he found out it was him.

Alexander Rolland (8)
Pentland Primary School, Edinburgh

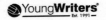

The Fat Cow

Once, there was a fat cow and let me tell you a tale. Let's start. For breakfast, Fatty had chocolate, doughnuts, sweets, Fanta, Irn-Bru, Pepsi Max, Coca-Cola and huge biscuits. Later, he went to town. Then he met someone fatter than him. So he went to the store with £5,000 and bought all the biggest foods they had.

When he got home he ate all of the food he had bought. He gobbled it all up. Mmm.

The next day, he went to town. He looked for the other fat guy that day and he was fatter. Yay.

Robert Hagarty (8)
Pentland Primary School, Edinburgh

The Flying Pig

It was one sunny day at Swanston Farm. All the pigs were rolling in the mud like usual, except for one unusual pig. You see, this pig could fly! Yes, fly! This pig didn't roll in the mud all day. He would fly, see the world, fight against lava monsters, and of course be on top. But this pig you see had the memory of a turtle! He may fly extremely fast but his brain was as slow as a turtle.
And then he fell! Look! There, he just fell. "Oh! Are you okay?" And Piggy was injured again...

Reese Robertson (8)
Pentland Primary School, Edinburgh

The Poorly Chef

Once, there was a chef who lived in a café. One day, he felt poorly. He made a bowl of pasta to make him feel better. He didn't like the bowl of pasta because he forgot to cook it. Then he cooked it and added cookie crumbs because he thought it would make it taste better. But it didn't. So he just lay in bed, thinking about what to do. All of his customers had left so he closed his shop. But there were still customers in the café. Later, he felt much better and saw the customers.

Cara Bisset (8)
Pentland Primary School, Edinburgh

Bouncing Bunny

Once upon a time, there was a bouncing bunny who was called Bouncing Bunny because she was so bouncy. One day she went on a walk to the forest and a very cool thing happened. Bouncing Bunny discovered how amazingly high she could jump. She could jump so high that she got stuck up a tree so the firemen came and they had a ladder made out of lollipops. Bouncing Bunny was hungry so she ate her way down and taught her baby sister how to jump high like her. Then her sister shouted, "Jump now!"

Ellie Lendrum (8)
Pentland Primary School, Edinburgh

The Hairy Hairdryer

One normal day at the hairdressers, a little girl came in. She was sooo hairy. My owner was shocked even though she had eleven-metre-long hair. When the girl left straight away weirdly she didn't mind. Then I got put in my drawer. I was sad but I got out secretly but set the stupid alarm off. I got back in my dumb box then my owner came to me and started hugging me because I was sooo special to her.

In the morning I woke up next to her. When she was open she gave me a haircut.

Autumn Edgar (8)
Pentland Primary School, Edinburgh

The Walking, Talking Toilet

One day, in one messy house, when you walked in the toilet you would see a walking, talking toilet. After I said hi to my toilet I said, "Do you want to watch TV with me?"

He said, "Yes." He wanted to watch other toilets and he loved to watch other toilets and it was minging but he didn't think it was minging.

So I went to bed but he followed me. So I went to the shops and he was scared to see other people so he stayed in the house and fell asleep.

Jayden Millar (8)
Pentland Primary School, Edinburgh

The Farting Policeman

A policeman was strolling in town until crime came. He only said, "You are..." And *puff!* He farted.

"Eww..." said the robber.

"Well, everyone farts," he said.

"But that is gross," said the robber. "It smells gross."

"Erm, no it does not. It smells like cake!"

"It really doesn't," said the robber.

"You, Mr, are going to jail!" said the farting policeman.

Eve McKenna (8)

Pentland Primary School, Edinburgh

Silly Toilet!

A boy was at home and he went to the toilet. He sat on the toilet and did his poops and when he'd done he couldn't really flush it! The boy got really angry at himself because he could not flush the toilet! So he asked his dad to come and help. His dad tried to flush the toilet and he thought it was easy. But the boy thought it was so hard but he also tried it again and it was super duper easy. So his dad was so mad because he thought he was lying to him!

Mohammad Ghanbari (8)
Pentland Primary School, Edinburgh

The Big Hairy Monster

One day there was a big hairy monster. He went to the monster shop. He waited on a seat then it was his shot. He got a hairy seat. He said, "Oh no! This means I am going to get more hair. I got all my annoying hair off." Then he only had hairy money and the guy was like why?

The monster walked home. When he got home he was tired so he went to sleep.

When he woke up there was hair all over him. He went back and got his hair off.

Otis Henderson (8)
Pentland Primary School, Edinburgh

The Crazy Sunglasses

Once there were crazy sunglasses. They lived in Turkey. It was very hot in Turkey so of course, the crazy sunglasses got very hot. Whenever the crazy sunglasses got ice cream they always melted. Crazy Sunglasses had to put sunscreen on every two seconds. Crazy Sunglasses got put on people's faces all the time! Even though Crazy Sunglasses put on sun cream every two seconds, Crazy Sunglasses melted.

Felicity Noble (8)

Pentland Primary School, Edinburgh

Big, Fat Baby

In the Land of Boom-Boom, there lived a big, fat baby. Everyone could only say Boom-Boom. The big, fat baby just managed to say wee wee and as soon as he said it the land melted into wee wee. King Boom came and told Chief Boom to put the big, fat baby in prison.
Two years later, the Land of Boom-Boom was now 99.9% boom and 0.1% wee.

Conor Sheridan (8)
Pentland Primary School, Edinburgh

Bunny Mischief

Did you know the Easter Bunny has an evil twin, Bunny Mischief? Mischief wanted to be the Easter Bunny so he plotted to do terrible things. The day before Easter, Mischief changed the calendar. He poured sleeping powder on the Easter Bunny's pillow. While he slept, Mischief delivered Easter eggs filled with slimy worms, bunny poop, beetle juice and tarantulas. Then he went to sleep as if nothing had happened.

In the morning, Easter Bunny saw that there were protests. The Bunny family found out it was Mischief who was responsible and killed him. They delivered yummy chocolate to everyone.

Olivia Fraser

Preston Tower Primary School, Prestonpans

Suspicious Shark

Unicorn Willie was walking along a beach. Suddenly a sausage popped up. Willie screamed! The sausage asked to play. Unicorn Willie thought, *is this my imagination?* They built sandcastles. A sponge jumped out of the sea and scared them. The sponge wanted to play. They splashed in the water. An egg appeared, they looked at each other in amazement. The egg played too. Then a shark came. They tried to get out of the water. The shark wanted to play but had a scary smile. They looked at each other and said, "Maybe tomorrow." They ran away really fast.

Calvin McBrierty
Preston Tower Primary School, Prestonpans

The Forgetful Chef

The forgetful chef worked in a Chinese restaurant.
A waiter asked him to cook chicken curry.
The chef said, "You don't tell me what to do. Just give me the paper that has the order on, okay!"
The boss came into the kitchen. He was very cross with the chef. He was about to fire him but another worker came into the kitchen and said, "The waiters are waiting for their chicken curry, hurry up and cook it." Everyone went back to work but the same thing happened again. The forgetful chef was fired and never got a job again.

Jay Brechin
Preston Tower Primary School, Prestonpans

The Hungry Superhero

One night, there was a very hungry superhero called Hungrily. Hungrily suddenly sat up in bed and said, "Oh, why did I eat my wife?" Didn't I tell you that he ate the whole Earth? So now he lives on the moon.

One day when Hungrily was just having a cuppa there was a little knock at the door. "I wonder who that could be." He went to the door and opened it and then a mouse kicked Hungrily off his feet. That's when the fight began. Hungrily said shyly, "How about we be friends?"

"Never!" the mouse cried loudly.

Niamh Aldis (10)
Preston Tower Primary School, Prestonpans

The Clumsy Chef

Once upon a time, there was an old haunted house. A chef named Jamie worked there, he was very clumsy. A naughty ghost called Gasper lived there too. Gasper would turn the lights off and make plates float in the air, scaring the customers. Gasper sometimes made Jamie trip and fall and spill food all over the customers. If Jamie burnt the food then Gasper would scream, "Quick, the house is going to burn down!"
Jamie had enough of Gasper's tricks and he warned him not to do this again. Gasper listened to Jamie and all the customers came back.

Abby McKenzie (10)
Preston Tower Primary School, Prestonpans

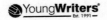

Peter, The Polite Polar Bear

She was staring at him again, her big blue eyes looking at him like something was very wrong. He was just trying to eat his sliced cucumber and tomato sandwiches in peace. His favourite thing to eat on a Sunday afternoon in the park. So Peter the polar bear decided to do something about it. He got up and stretched out his paws and slowly padded over to the little girl. He opened his wide jaws. The girl's eyes grew even wider.

"Do you want to share my picnic?" asked Peter. The little girl smiled widely. "Yes, please!" she answered.

Abigail Shearer
Preston Tower Primary School, Prestonpans

The Evil Football

One day, I was playing football when I started to feel weird. The feeling was tingly like someone was watching me. I looked at the football; it had a mouth and eyes! The mouth opened and tried to bite me. It jumped out of my hands and rolled. Soon it was rolling after everyone. People were running and screaming. The football was crazy. When we tried kicking it, it would bite our feet. Luckily, its teeth weren't that sharp but I didn't like it. I kicked the football really hard and it disappeared into the sky. We were safe.

Daniel Cormack
Preston Tower Primary School, Prestonpans

The Hungry Toilet

In the restaurant there was a strange toilet in cubicle number two. The toilet rolls always seemed to go missing. Could the toilet be eating them? I went to investigate. I could hear gurgling noises coming from the cubicle and then a massive burp! When I entered I could see a pair of feet sticking out. The toilet was eating a customer! Could the toilet really be that hungry? I decided to get out of there fast. I hope the people who were eaten managed to escape to the sea and I hope the toilet rolls don't pollute the sea.

Lucy Thomson (10)
Preston Tower Primary School, Prestonpans

The Crazy Football

I was playing in my garden, practising my football skills. I was kicking my ball very high, trying to get my best score when suddenly the ball zoomed over the fence.

I heard a man shout, "Ouch!" My ball had hit him on the head by accident. I thought the man would give me a telling off so I hid. The man shouted over the fence, "Who did that?"

I told him I was very sorry and he gave my ball back. I decided to play with my scooter instead. I put my crazy football safely away in the shed.

Cody Murphy (10)
Preston Tower Primary School, Prestonpans

Evil Tomato

Evil Tomato tried every day to escape the shop but he was never able to because there were too many people coming and going. He tried on days the shop was closed, but the windows and doors were locked. Every other vegetable waited, still on the shelves, until they got chosen. The evil tomato tried to push them off the shelves.

One day the owner forgot to shut the window. Evil Tomato saw his chance. He rolled as fast as he could and dropped out. A man's foot came down on top of him and he was squished!

Cayden Lawson (10)

Preston Tower Primary School, Prestonpans

The Evil Doctor

There once lived a man called Armor who worked as a doctor. He had a little girl called Lilly. Lilly was very nice but her dad was very mean. Armor once had to pull someone's heart out and replace it. There was a lot of blood and it was gross. Since that day, he has been an evil doctor.

One day he had to give a patient a flu vaccination but since he was the evil doctor he gave her the wrong vaccination on purpose. Luckily, the patient saw the bottle and called the police. Armor went to jail forever.

Fabiana Ferreira
Preston Tower Primary School, Prestonpans

Pumping Cat Pizza

One pumping cat pizza day, I was sitting watching TV in a good mood. Suddenly a pumping cat pizza came out of nowhere. Suddenly it started jumping around and pumping everywhere around the house. It was so annoying. I could not pan the pizza. After that, I started to get a little freaked when it was pulling his pepperoni off! I quickly ran and screamed, "No! Stop!" Then it stopped. I took it off the table and said, "Who are you?"
He said, "I'm your cat, Sami. I got stuck in this yesterday."

Ala Mazurek (10)
St Mungo's RC Primary School, Alloa

The Forgetful Superhero

One day, there was a superhero that was really forgetful. He was watching TV. He was watching Maleficent. Suddenly, his phone rang. He grabbed it out of his pocket and answered it. He needed to save somebody. Straight away, he flew to the fighting scene. He got there and then something forgetful happened. He thought, *Oh no. I forgot what to do.* That's the thing about being one of the most forgetful people in the world. He went back to his house and continued casually watching TV like nothing had happened.

Martin de Vries (10)
St Mungo's RC Primary School, Alloa

The Lonely Leaf

Greeno is a leaf. Not long ago, he fell from the old oak tree. Greeno struggles to make new friends so today he wanted to speak to the twigs. He was walking towards the twigs when he tripped on a bit of dirt. Greeno looked up to see... Mr Tomato. This was not who he wanted to see. Mr Tomato helped him up and asked Greeno if he was okay. Greeno didn't reply as he glanced around, hoping to see the twigs. They weren't there. Greeno decided to make friends with Mr Tomato. Before long, they were best friends!

Eve Louise Blyth (10)
St Mungo's RC Primary School, Alloa

Clumsy Ghost

Jeff the ghost flew over the grass and saw a junkyard. There was metal and squashed cars. Jeff thought it was a playground. He bumped into everything. It was in very neat piles until Jeff came. The manager was wondering who was doing this and came down from the building. There were so so many stairs. The manager could not get through the rubbish and metal. Then a car came flying towards him and he jumped out the way. It just missed him. Jeff heard footsteps so he quickly ran and tidied everything he could.

Jamie MacAskill (10)
St Mungo's RC Primary School, Alloa

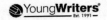

The Fish That Couldn't Fly

This is a story about a flying fish that couldn't fly. So on the day of his first flying lesson he came in wearing a bikini! Small see-through wings poked out at his back. Everybody stared.

"Right," the coach began, "today we are going to teach you how to fly."

The fish that couldn't fly jumped off the springboard then he fell flat on his face. He was so embarrassed he let out an enormous smelly fart. The fart was so strong it took him all the way to Timbuktu!

Isla Mullan (10)
St Mungo's RC Primary School, Alloa

Crazy Kangaroo

The kangaroo can't jump so he climbs a lot. His friends can jump perfectly and Crazy Kangaroo gets jealous. So he tries to make a huge machine that jumps for him. He takes it out for a spin but it explodes and breaks.

So a few weeks later, he gives up until he sees a wand and he gets an idea. He buys a magic book and tries and tries until *poof!* He can jump and he jumps and jumps. So he runs to his friends and says, "I can jump!" and he jumps!

Matthew Little (10)
St Mungo's RC Primary School, Alloa

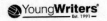

The Human That Didn't Like People

One day, Barf had to wake up for swimming class. He hated people so he didn't participate. After class, his mum said, "We're gonna go to the beach tomorrow."
So the next day, Barf went to the market to get a mask so nobody could see his face. When he got there he just sat on the towels. Then his nose was getting bigger and bigger until... he ran to his mum to tell her but as soon as he got out the shade his clothes changed and his arm got longer!

Samavia Javeed (9)
St Mungo's RC Primary School, Alloa

The Trumping Chips!

One bright cloudless day, I was in the car with my mum and dad going to McDonald's. On the way there we listened to good tunes. When we got there we got three drinks and three packets of chips because we weren't that hungry. When I saw my packet I heard a noise and there was not a nice smell. Then I saw my chips running away from me as well as farting. I was so stunned I did not eat them and I put them in the bin when I got home.

Lucy Barr (10)

St Mungo's RC Primary School, Alloa

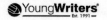

The Grumbling Rabbit

Once upon a time, there was a rabbit who was having a peaceful sleep when suddenly he was woken up by the sound of someone cutting down his tree. He couldn't get back to sleep so he decided to move into the bushes. When he got there he went to sleep.

He woke up very fast because the fire alarm went off so he had to leave. He was so fed up that he got on a boat to Scotland where he could sleep in peace.

Aidan Lambert (10)
St Mungo's RC Primary School, Alloa

The Story Of G Ghost

The Gangsta Ghost lived in a street called Gangsta Street but Gangsta Ghost was different. He kept farting and he was invisible so the people just randomly heard farting noises so they moved out. Gangsta Ghost lived in the toilet.

One day, Gangsta Ghost had other plans. He took some glasses and a hat that had a G on it and became a proper gangster and got a tattoo somehow and lived in the air forever.

Dima Clark (11)

St Mungo's RC Primary School, Alloa

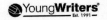

Crazy Pumpy Poopy Pants

I was sitting on the toilet minding my own business, doing my business. Then a poo came out of my butt and went crazy. The poo was being really annoying so I tried to flush it down the toilet but it wouldn't go down the toilet. So I decided to eat my poo but I had to put him or her in the oven. I set the table and then started to eat the poo but for two weeks I was pooping non-stop!

Hannah McMillan (9)
St Mungo's RC Primary School, Alloa

The Trumping Teacher

One day like any other, I was going into school. Then I saw my teacher bending forward and *woof!* It came. A stinking fart. The whole class squealed and burst out laughing. The teacher said, "Oh, I didn't see you there. On to your task."
For the whole day, it went on and on. By the end of the day the class stank. I went home and had a shower instantly.

Macy Ireland (10)
St Mungo's RC Primary School, Alloa

YoungWriters®

The Magical Kitchen

Once, a potion spilled all over a cookie. Then... *pop!* It came alive! "Hello, anyone here?" said the cookie. She started to look around.

"Hey, do you wanna be my friend?" asked Cute Cookie.

"No!" said Brocolli. "You're not healthy!"

"Aww, man!" said Cute Cookie. She came across a lemon. She looked sad. "Are you okay?" asked Cute Cookie.

"No," said Lemon.

"Wanna be my friend?" asked Cute Cookie.

"Yes!" said Lemon.

They took a walk around the kitchen but... the kitchen flew up into the sky above. People were pointing and screaming. "Uh, what?" said Lemon and Cute Cookie.

Hanin Alqarni (8)
Thornwood Primary School, Glasgow

The Grotty Teacher

On the first day of school, a teacher called Miss Chavysnunz joined the school. At first, she was nice. Then after term two, she said things like, "Get my coffee!" Everyone started to hate her... Once, she even farted in someone's face and she meant to!

Someone got payback. He went into the ladies' staff toilets and got a big bucket of toilet water and as soon as Miss Chavysnunz entered the bathroom the student splashed the water all over her new 'expensive' clothes! Miss Chavysnunz was super angry so she flushed him down the toilet! Now he's a frog.

Freya Stewart (9)
Thornwood Primary School, Glasgow

Agent Granny!

A long time ago, before the police were around, there was a small teahouse. The teahouse was very close to the chippy, so that meant the teahouse was quite popular. In fact, it was so popular the old folks would go have tea every day! There was Ann, Margaret, Rosemary and Bill. But one day something very suspicious happened. Ann's teabag went missing! That made Ann angry so she turned into Agent Granny and she was ready for a fight. She checked everyone's stinky pockets but one wasn't stinky... Bill's! She took it and Granny was fuming!

Cal Hanlon (9)
Thornwood Primary School, Glasgow

124

The Evil Brother And Nice Sister

Long ago lived an evil brother and a nice sister. The evil brother was very bad. He would steal and break his sister's toys and call her by horrible names.

One day, the sister went to take a bath. Suddenly the bathtub started to lift. The sister was screaming, "Arghh! Arghh!" Then she noticed it was her evil brother. She was thinking, *where will it go?*

She floated down the river and landed on Easter Island. She met the Easter Bunny and stayed there forever. She didn't miss her evil brother at all!

Iona Sherrington (8)

Thornwood Primary School, Glasgow

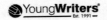

The Stinky Chef

There was a chef and he was really stinky. One time he made soup and he really needed a fart. So he took the bowl of soup, put it on the ground and sat down on the soup and farted. He took it to the person who wanted the soup. But the person didn't know that he'd farted on it.

When the chef gave the bowl to the person they smelled the soup. The person was sick all over the restaurant. He shouted, "Everyone, get out!" Everyone got out. Everyone called him names. So the chef ran away in sadness.

Robbie Sawatzky (8)
Thornwood Primary School, Glasgow

Evil Teacher

Today we had a new teacher... She seemed quite nice... at first. However, when the bell rang for playtime and we went outside to play, our teacher, Miss Lee, did not go to the staffroom. I saw her sneak into the art cupboard. When she came out she had a coloured mouth. The bell rang. We lined up. Miss Lee looked really suspicious.

At home time we were spying on her. She went into the art cupboard again. This time she drank the potion that us pupils made... She turned into an ant and we squished her!

Aqsa Ahmad (8)
Thornwood Primary School, Glasgow

The Family With The Stinkiest Toilet!

In a town called Dumbling Dum lived a family called Laziest Laze. All the family was bald. They did a lot of embarrassing things like going to the airport in their undies because their clothes were rainbow (they hate rainbows). Or like yesterday at the supermarket when the dad did an enormous fart! But the worst thing about the family was... the toilet. The stinkiest thing in the house! The toilet was sad. The only thing he wanted was their business! The owners did their business under their beds!

Stefanie Kokkinaki (9)
Thornwood Primary School, Glasgow

Poorly Ninja

Speeding through the red light, farting as he drove, Ninja had a windy emergency. When Ninja arrived at the hospital all the people were having a broken bone party. He walked into the hospital and started to dance to the music and farted.
Everybody looked at him and sniffed it. Everyone said, "That was a juicy one." Everybody started to fart and dance to the music.
Poorly Ninja had to go back to his room. The doctor gave him some fart medicine. He started to fart even more!

Logan Gow (8)
Thornwood Primary School, Glasgow

The Hairy Monster

He was a hairy monster. He lived in a hairy and stinky old house. He made everyone in the world have so much hair by using evil hairy powers. His magical friend gave him power and when he gave people more hair their hair turned into whatever they wanted. When he did that the people called him a very good friend and made him the king. He gave them all the things that they wanted. He was so happy that he was the king and gave the people anything they wanted until they died.

Ibrahim Nazir (8)
Thornwood Primary School, Glasgow

Agent Bacon

One time there was an agent called Mr Bacon and he was planning a top-secret mission to steal the golden roll of toilet paper. He went to his secret hideout to plan his theft.

At night he went to the bank when suddenly he was caught by security. But he had a trick up his sleeve. He had rolls and bacon! He snuck into the vault then made his way in. "Into the vault I go," he said.

Then he sold the golden roll and bought ten million rolls and bacon!

Kieran Alcorn (8)
Thornwood Primary School, Glasgow

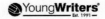

Cookie Chaos

The cookies, Missomi and Animie, were baked in South Korea. They got shipped to the UK and got bought and eaten! They had an adventure! They slid down a pineapple (I did not know there were pineapples in my body) and they played catch with a kidney (sounds better now). They didn't realise that they slept in stomach acid! They found a muffin friend and a way out (don't tell me). They were in a swimming pool, it was yellow and dark with long brown things!

Anna Marie McShane (9)
Thornwood Primary School, Glasgow

The Jealous Ninja

At gym the jealous ninja got an F- for doing bad ninja moves. He was very angry that he got an F-. He said to himself, "I wish I was not here at all." And that was what he did. He never went to Ninja School ever again.

The only thing he was good at was boxing but he was not in boxing class. One night, he snuck to the boxing class. He was very excited to do boxing skills in class. He got an A+ for the first time in his entire life.

Nampreet Kaur Brar (8)
Thornwood Primary School, Glasgow

Mean Miss Riches

Once in a faraway school called Sweaty Man
Primary, there was a teacher. Her name was Miss
Riches. She was mean and when it was her turn to
teach Class One she asked a question and a
student got the answer wrong. That kid would get
a severe punishment!
At lunch when the teachers went to the staffroom,
Miss Riches would not. So two students from Class
One, Amie and Sam, went to check it out... You
wouldn't believe what they saw!

Mabel Elizabeth Gurney (8)
Thornwood Primary School, Glasgow

The Lazy Toilet

Long ago in a toilet forest, there was a lazy toilet who was very lazy and clumsy. His friends called him Lazynosey, Lazypants and Lazyfarts. It was so mad he felt like calling names back but he was too lazy so he just phoned them instead. But they told the king. He was mad. He was very strong. He made him work for him. He was so mad he didn't like it. He apologised to the king. The king let him go. He had a good life after.

Harsimran Kaur Sohal (8)
Thornwood Primary School, Glasgow

Gangsta Ninja

At night time Gangsta Ninja broke into a bank store and started robbing the bank store. Meanwhile, he got so excited that he got caught in the security cameras and he didn't even notice that he got caught in the cameras. He got so carried away that he started making funny faces at the security cameras. They put him in jail and he farted all over the place so they took him out of jail and put him into fart jail.

Navneet Brar (9)
Thornwood Primary School, Glasgow

Happy Pizza

Yesterday a pizza came alive! The pizza came alive from a small microwave in the dinner hall. The pizza liked to cause trouble every day. In the dinner hall it was Burger vs Pizza. Pizza won! Then the dinner hall shut down.

There was a boy called Fart Nugget. He farted on the pizza. He farted every twenty seconds. He was obsessed with burgers. He farted on Pizza and Pizza died.

Matthew Fletcher (8)
Thornwood Primary School, Glasgow

Big Barfing Bowel

This story is embarrassing, as it's mostly true. It's also quite disgusting. The taming of the poo.
It started, oh, quite innocent, with the daily chore. The flushing of one's bowels, unaware of what lay in store. Looking down, I felt quite ill from what lay down in the wake like a cork. It bobbed about. I flushed again. The water swirled. It went round and round. But when the water became still there was floating mould. I piled it with paper, in hope to make it go down. Another flush would do the trick, as the water gurgled down.

Teagan Jagger (12)
Winton Primary School, Ardrossan

YOUNG WRITERS
INFORMATION

We hope you have enjoyed reading this book – and
that you will continue to in the coming years.

If you're a young writer who enjoys reading and creative
writing, or the parent of an enthusiastic poet or story writer,
do visit our website **www.youngwriters.co.uk**. Here you
will find free competitions, workshops and games, as well
as recommended reads, a poetry glossary and our blog.
There's lots to keep budding writers motivated to write!

If you would like to order further copies of this book,
or any of our other titles, then please give us a
call or order via your online account.

Young Writers
Remus House
Coltsfoot Drive
Peterborough
PE2 9BF
(01733) 890066
info@youngwriters.co.uk

Join in the conversation!
Tips, news, giveaways and much more!

 YoungWritersUK   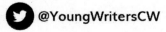 @YoungWritersCW